For Dan,

I have missed you every day since you left us.
Until the next life, my love.

BLOOD ON THE ROSES

BLOOD ON THE ROSES

BRENDA W. BACON

Chateau Bacon Press, LLC

1

Candyman

I was just a girl of twenty, but I was no child. I had already lived a lifetime, having buried both my parents while still a teenager. A mere girl of twenty, who had already sold her body and gave freely of her soul to anyone with a nice smile.

He was a man of nearly seventy.

When I first saw him, I was somewhat repulsed. His tattered clothes and dirty felt hat. His coarse hands, cracked from the kind of work my soft generation and those who came after would never abide doing. He was tall and awkward, like a puppy confused by its limbs. But he was no puppy. He was ancient.

Everything about him, from his features to his accent, seemed exaggerated, as if he were a caricature.

I mostly ignored him and went about my duties, wrapping bouquets and ringing up the sales. In the little office behind the register the old man sat, amiably chattering away with the boss's son.

I loved my job, working all day with my hands and creating beautiful things. I'd started there just before Christmas, to help with the rush. I must have done a pretty good job – though prying a compliment out of either the boss or the Greek who managed the place would have been impossible – because they asked me to stay on full time. I much preferred it to working in a stuffy office, with the same routine day after day. But my income didn't meet my outgoings. An off-hand remark to the boss one day snowballed into an alternate career, one conducted in secrets and shadows.

We were by ourselves in the little office. His kids were elsewhere, the Greek in the greenhouse, and I was preparing a bouquet for delivery. The boss had been flirting, as men of a certain age will do, and while I worked I tossed "That'll cost you!" over my shoulder to him, clearly joking around.

"How much?" Suddenly serious. He called my bluff. I could have backed down, but that wasn't my style. Besides, I needed the money. I had to follow through. I did some calculations in my head, named a price. He countered. We negotiated. Set a time. And that was that. I became a whore.

As he was my only client for some time, I guess a better term might have been "paid mistress," but that was just semantics.

Selling my body wasn't much of a leap for me. At twenty I had had a few partners, none of whom I particularly liked. In almost every case, I traded my body for something in return: companionship, revenge, a means to an end. Even the loss of my virginity at 14 was a trade-off: either accept that I was going to have sex, or the boy I was with would hit me. With my mother already ravaged by cancer, it was easier to acquiesce than it was to seek help. There were far more important things happening at home, after all.

When it came to sex, hard currency was a far cleaner trade, with clear parameters and a time limit. Spending an hour with my boss now and then for an agreed-upon price did not bleed into my day-to-day existence, although I know it made him nervous. One indiscreet word at work, and his life would collapse. I could always get a new job. He couldn't get a new family.

It made me laugh that if any of my friends ever found out about my arrangement, they would pooh-pooh it as wrong. Funny that they themselves would give their bodies to strangers they met in a bar but couldn't imagine charging a fee to a gentleman they were somewhat fond of.

And I *was* fond of him. He was an attractive older man, Italian stock, with flashing dark eyes of the sort I generally fell for anyway. He was appreciative of my body, and we took pleasure from each other. Also, he wasn't a bad guy to work for. In the days since, I've worked for some shady characters, and I'd love to go back in time to work for him – under any circumstance.

He was lonely. His wife would spend the cold winters far from Buffalo, sunning and golfing in West Palm Beach, while he toiled away in the city, keeping the business running. Purchasing an hour's worth of company was far tidier than bringing a girlfriend into the mix and risking his home. Sometimes we just went out for dinner or a drink, nothing more. However, in retrospect, I'm sure we're both glad that we got away with our temporary arrangement. The old adage "don't shit where you eat" certainly should have applied.

My friendship with his daughter was a source of discomfort for him and me both. He wanted me to stop having dinner with her at the cheap pasta place down the road, and playing pool with her on evenings off. It was inappropriate, he said. I laughed and reminded him that I had far more invested in my friendship with his daughter than in my relationship with him, and that as far as "inappropriate" went, I didn't think he had the moral wherewithal to make that judgment.

We kept our workplace détente, and I never breathed a word.

The strange old man with the long legs and the funny hat would visit our little shop every few days, and either huddle out in the greenhouse with the Greek as he labored over some device or other, or sit on the counter in the little office to chat with whoever was working. Not me, though. It was as if he didn't even see me. I thought he was stand-offish, or that he didn't expect me to last working there, so there was no point in even being polite to me. I later learned he was just painfully shy.

The boss's children, she my age and he a little older, worked in tandem with me and spoke often of someone named Hans, but I had no idea who that was. A customer? A supplier, more likely. The boss had an attractive middle-aged friend who drove a flashy car. For a while I was under the impression that this was the Hans person the kids talked about. Naturally at no point did I suspect this friendly sounding Hans character could be the elderly vagabond.

One late winter day after I had begun my affair with the boss, the old man came in while I was alone. The Greek was running errands, the son was at lunch, the boss was in Florida, and his daughter had the day off. I was on my own. We had never really spoken, he and I. The occasional "excuse me" or "thanks" was the extent of our converse. Now suddenly I was alone with this strange man. He gave me the creeps.

Seeing that it was just the two of us, I suppose he felt a little trapped. It would be rude to flee, yet I could tell he had no desire to talk to me. However, being of a gentlemanly sort, he smiled and did his best. And like the villain from the after-school specials I had been raised on, he reached into his jacket and pulled out a yellow lollipop. "You want a candy?"

I eyed him skeptically, and narrowed my eyes. "Red." He reached back in and pulled out a handful, from which I plucked the desired red one. Cherry.

I won't pretend I remember what uncomfortable small talk we made to fill the silence. I was surprised he even stayed to talk. I guess he was just hoping that the Greek would hurry back and rescue him from having to sit with this strange girl. He left within the hour, before the boss's son even made it back from lunch. I didn't want to insult him, as he was clearly a friend of the family, but it bothered me to have him around.

He returned in his usual pattern of semi-random days. I saw him a lot as we progressed into a wet early spring. I had wised to the fact that this apparition was indeed the mysterious Hans, an Austro-Hungarian of indeterminate age who fled to our country in a time of war. The pieces fell in place for me one Sunday morning in late March, when we were unexpectedly hit with a heavy snowstorm. The boss's daughter and I fought our respective ways into the store that day and parked in the nearby shopping center lot. Trudging through the drifts, we made it into the warm store, and she immediately called Hans for help. Within 30 minutes, the old man and his plow arrived to clear us out. He even valeted our cars from the nearby lot to the front of the store so we wouldn't have to climb back over snowbanks to get to them. So that was Hans. Huh.

Also, he always brought me cherry red lollipops after that first day.

One warm day in early May, we were receiving the rose bushes. Though most of the time the shop functioned as a florist, in the summer it also became a garden center. The courtyard would hold racks of annual flats, and pile after pile of bagged soil and manure. We the worker bees would haul all this stuff to customers' cars thanklessly, as tipping was neither encouraged nor did it ever actually happen. At least I got a good workout from it.

I had been called in on my off Wednesday to tag the prickly wooden stumps that jutted from the peat pots the Greek had put them in. I was resentful of giving up my one day off. I knew that with Mother's Day coming, and then spring planting, I wouldn't be seeing many more days off till the end of summer. Scowling, I went about the tagging. As an act of rebellion, I wore clothes I knew the boss would disapprove of: Torn jeans and a loose tank top. He felt these – especially the tank – were completely inappropriate attire for a female. Unfortunately, he wasn't in that morning, so he never saw my defiance. And the Greek didn't care, so long as the work got done. I could have stood there naked, and the only thing he would have said would be "You're going to get cut up."

Eventually Hans appeared and dug in next to the Greek. My small female hands were ideally suited to the detailed work of moving between the thorns and tagging the bushes, and I moved fast, though I bled a lot. The thorns had torn me over and over, yet I worked ever faster, eager to start my day off as soon as possible. I had no idea just how many breeds and hybrids there were until I saw the stacks of tags. A dozen or so of one hybrid, ten of another. The task seemed insurmountable, but I was determined to get out of there by lunchtime. I kept outpacing my duo of surly companions. "Hurry up!" I'd call to them. "Getting bored over here!" I'd tease. They spoke to each other in the male language of grunts and hand gestures, the Greek chain-smoking his way to an early grave and the old man defying death with activity.

I was shocked to see that these two men didn't even bother with gloves while grabbing hold of the stumps and plopping the roots into pots. I bled, they didn't. Again, I was struck by the years of work that contributed to the calluses that protected them. I looked down at my own bloody palms – a florist's stigmata – and thought of how different I was from them. Even though the boss's daughter had worked there since she was a kid, her hands remained soft. She and I were shielded from any real work of the kind the Greek was doing.

It was just past noon when we finished, and the courtyard was overflowing with rosebushes, in rows of ten, over a hundred pots deep. We had completed over one thousand bushes in what I'm told was just slightly more than half the time of the previous year. To date, I hold the shop's record for fastest tagger.

It was the bloody labor that day which earned me something I didn't know I was missing or even needed: the old man's respect. My silent efficiency esteemed me in his eyes. His was a generation of sacrifice, and seeing someone work –

and bleed – silently and without complaint was worthy of his respect. Little did he know how much I resented being there that morning.

I bear the scars of roses to this day. I carry them with me, and each one is a memory.

When I wasn't making bouquets or on outdoor duty, I was below stairs most days, preparing the thousands of flowers we received each week. Ours was a shop where top quality flowers were sold at bargain prices, due to our buying them in bulk direct from the growers. Every week, usually on a Tuesday morning, we received multiple crates of roses, mums, carnations and assorted in-season blossoms. The store was known for roses, and that's what we had the most of. The two walk-in fridges held bundle after bundle of them, straight from Bogotá. Every imaginable hue, from snow white to black red. Black roses are a rare phenomenon, occurring when red pigment is high. Like blood. We treasured each one as you might a four-leaf clover. We never sold them.

Occasionally the Greek or the boss's son would work in the basement with me, pulling a hand rake through the bundles, ripping leaves and thorns off, leaving room for the stems to sit without rot in warm water. Most of the time though, I worked in solitude, raking and snipping, and putting the blooms in warm water to gently open.

Past his shyness and realizing I wasn't so bad; Hans began to visit me in the cool dungeon I had been banished to. I had become used to his quiet weirdness by this time and welcomed the distraction from the long hours of solitary confinement. He would wordlessly pick up the rake and begin to work across from me at the sturdy tack table where I stood for so many hours. He would bypass his longtime friends up in the shop to work, without pay or even thanks, with me. After a while, as he raked and I clipped, he began to talk to me.

I had learned from my masters above stairs that the old man was anything but the hobo he appeared to be. Upon arrival in the United States, he immediately set himself up as a gardener and landscaper, having brought nothing with him from the old country except a girl and a knowledge of farming. His fortunes grew with hard work, planting gardens in the summer and plowing snow in the cold Buffalo winters. That's how he came to know the boss, back when they were both young bucks, working in landscaping and manual labor. Though my boss was also blessed with having sold a good deal of his family's farmland to a large pharmaceutical company (which shall not be named, but whose famous product featured in my relationship with him), which gave him a financial head start Hans didn't have. While my boss was able to invest his money and move into a smaller, less labor-intensive business his daughter could one day run, the old man chose to keep plugging away. Despite the hard work, or likely because of it, he stayed young while my boss grew old and embraced semi-retirement.

With a typical European distrust of banks, it was rumored his wealth – accumulated over five decades – was stashed within the walls of his home. He was teased relentlessly by the Greek, who always threatened to someday pull up his floorboards.

Though I was intrigued by his old clothes and Howard Hughes eccentricities, for once my mind wasn't given over to its usual avarice. The real wealth came from what he carried with him: the past.

The time and place he hailed from was well-documented and taught to every school child around the world with the admonishment *Never Again*. Yet I had heard the stories of only one side. The stories of the lucky few who remained. I had never been able to sit and talk with someone from the side of evil. The side defeated by the Allies. I tried to take it all in without judgment, but that wasn't so easy to do.

I'm not sure what I expected when he began to tell me of his past. Hatred and supremacy, I supposed. Yet what I got instead surprised me. All those years of heart-rending lessons of the Shoah, images of the starving prisoners, the bodies in wall-high piles by open mass graves, and no one bothered to mention that the average German suffered, too. While the angry little narcissist threw parades and made speeches, those in the country who had never even met a Jew, let alone learned to hate them, were starving under war-induced deprivations.

In the lessons I'd learned, all the Germans were equally guilty. But the tales that were taught to me were of grown men in uniform doing heinous things and hiding behind the excuse of "just following orders." We weren't taught about the non-militarized Germans. It wasn't until I got out of school and started actually learning something that I found out the Russians may have been just as inherently evil than the force they fought. The raping and killing of women and children, the abuses on the dead, the whole Ostfront was a horror. But out in the countryside, on the struggling farms, most Germans just wanted the whole nightmare over. Two wars in less than a generation was two too many.

Austria had barely recovered from the Great War by the time Hitler rose to glory. The wars must have run together for some. Roads were still rutted where cannon wagons had destroyed them. Families had lost sons and fathers, and there were only the young and the old left. Mines still dotted the countryside. Hans told me of being a boy working in the field with his grandfather. A click. The old man blown to bits and the boy screaming.

His eyes were so far away, and I knew he was reliving the moment. I knew he could see and smell every detail of the film his memory was replaying. Every horrifying detail. What do you say to that? What could I, a Gen-X kid raised in the softness and security of the suburbs, possibly offer up that could console? How could I even make the noises that said I understood? Sure, I'd lost my parents when I was very young, and to a wasting disease, but in the first world that was completely acceptable. I watched them die horribly, but in a manner approved by the society in which I was raised. Disease claimed you. Too much excess – of cigarettes and booze –

killed you. War didn't. Mines didn't. As Hans told me the fragments of the story that he could bear to say aloud, all I could do was listen.

We talked quietly, and I felt no need to comment. If I spoke, my words were soft, my laughter gentle and sincere when called for at all. He traded work and his stories for a little company. We were both lonely and found a measure of happiness in each other's friendship.

He opened up to me and was honest about where he'd been and what he'd seen in his seven decades on earth. War. Death. Hunger. Love. Women. Fear. He wanted nothing more than a safe, secure life in the New World, leaving behind the desolation of a homeland known throughout my short lifetime only for having spawned the devil. I listened without interruption, his words a gift. I accepted them as such and basked in his openness.

Week after week he came to me and me alone. Whatever they must have thought upstairs in the shop was of no concern to either of us. He was eccentric at best, so they were welcome to speculate. As I toiled away below stairs, he shared his life with me.

My own life interested him too: orphaned at sixteen, an only child, I stayed under the radar of the courts and worked different jobs to make ends meet. I didn't elaborate on what those jobs might entail.

I made no apologies and asked no favors. I wanted to work for my crumbs – even such work for such crumbs. My life was what it was, and I accepted it, just trying to survive each day. I was a rudderless child, scared and alone, as he once was. There was nothing separating us but time. So much time. A divide that could never be crossed, lest a life ending bring the cold breath of death to one only just beginning her life.

He called me Monica – pronounced Mone-ee-ka in his heavy accent – after the *scandale du jour* in 1998. I bore a passing resemblance to the chubby intern with the stylish bob, though my eyes didn't have the same dead look hers did. I suppose had my misdeeds been broadcast for all the world to devour, I too may have looked dead inside. It was a mercy that Hans could make the joke without knowing how much truth there was to it. Some things he was better off not knowing. I sometimes chuckled to myself at being nicknamed after the giver of the world's most famous blowjob. What would they say if they knew? My truest resemblance to Monica was best kept to myself.

Summer passed. My tan deepened from working out of doors; from getting out of the basement. Hans was busy with his landscaping clients, but still found time to pop in once or twice a week. My arms grew strong and sinewy from the lifting and hauling. Many of the cuts on my hands healed without being reopened time and again, as they had when I was strictly working with the flowers.

Over the summer, my most enjoyable times came close to

the end of the day. I would kick off my sandals and go barefoot out to the courtyard to water the pots and flats, as well as our little private patch of garden the Greek had planted. He was growing peppers and tomatoes. The boss's daughter and I would go out there every day and grab whatever little cherry tomatoes were ripe, eating them in the office with salt, juice squirting everywhere.

As the heat of the day abated, I would let all my worries and cares fall away as I watered. I saw nothing and heard nothing. There was only me and the abundance of plants and flowers around me. For those few minutes every day, I could forget that the shop sat at a busy intersection, with cars going by at all hours. I could forget a lot of things.

The months went by too fast, and summer left us. Roses again gave way to the pinecones, collected in half a dozen heavy trash liners, needing glittered and wired for the Christmas centerpieces that would soon be created to sit on tables across the city.

I sat cross-legged on the basement floor and he on a low hard-backed chair of the kind my elementary school teachers had sat on. Our hands cramped as we twisted the floral wire around the fat bottoms of the cones. Take a cone out of one bag, twist the wire once, twice, and then throw it into a new bag. They couldn't all be done in a day. It was an ongoing project through the Fall, a few hours at a time when there were no other chores and the shop wasn't busy.

It was quieter than at other times; autumn had no floral holidays. Sure, a few people picked up something if they were on their way to a Thanksgiving dinner, and our pots of colorful chrysanthemums sold well at this time of year, but we didn't sell as many roses as we normally did. If I wanted basement time, I worked on the cones.

I had grown to like the lonely basement work. For an hour or two every day, I could be by myself, quiet, no distractions. It was meditative to work with the flowers or pinecones while my mind cleared itself. My thoughts could wander, or if I was lucky, they would be still. Of course, having Hans made it better. We didn't always talk; sometimes we just methodically worked together in silence. I was comfortable being quiet with Hans in a way that I only wished I could be comfortable in silence with myself.

Come Christmas, the boss's daughter and the Greek would be busy sticking pine branches and candles into green floral foam and decorating the centerpieces with berries and these very cones. While they did that, I'd be creating Christmas bouquets and giant gold bows to decorate them with.

Bows. My toughest learning curve. The boss and the Greek all but gave up on my chance of ever learning how to loop the ribbons around my thumb and middle finger to create the bows that went in basket gardens and on presentation bouquets. I was pretty hopeless. The boss's daughter brought all the ugliest, unusable floral ribbon up from the basement, and she sat with me for hours on quiet Sundays, looping, twisting and snipping with me till I finally – after months – managed a ribbon that didn't look like a silky tangle of pasta. I like to think she'd be pleased to know I can still make them as beautifully as she patiently taught me.

While we wired the cones, Hans told me of his Gerda, the woman he escaped Europe with. He said he wasn't quite eighteen at the time, and she a year or two older. His mother didn't want him to go but knew that a better life waited. Gerda promised to care for him. Half a century later, they still lived together in a house by the lake. He admitted he had been unkind and unfaithful over the years, but he loved her still. "I only hope I go first. I couldn't bear losing her."

They never married; he was vague about it. There were no children, yet they had been together over half a century. He considered my boss's children to be like his own, since he'd been there when they were babies. But for himself, the blood ended there in the man who sat across from me.

"We learned English at the movies," he told me. In the afternoons, he and Gerda would take in a matinee – they were partial to Humphrey Bogart – and by watching the same movie over and over, they were able to learn rudimentary English. It was an ingenious idea.

In late November, we cleaned the last detritus of summer out of the courtyard: bags of soil, pallets of sheep manure, large scale garden implements. All of this went in the basement annex for next year, making room in the courtyard for the Christmas trees.

As much as I enjoyed working outside in the summer, I dreaded the Christmas trees in the winter. We sold different sized trees on a scale of prices, and we had to cart them and tie them to our customers' cars. Or worse yet, try to stuff them in trunks or the backs of minivans. All this meant getting our hands and clothes covered in the sticky sap which, as it turns out, I was mildly allergic to. On top of the mess of needles and goo, I was also sneezing incessantly! My eyes were red and puffy like I had a permanent head cold, and my wrists and the backs of my hands itched where the pine needles had scratched me.

Well, it wasn't all bad. It did smell terrific, after all.

The previous year I had bought one in time for my Christmas party and received many compliments about my beautifully decorated tree. This year though would be far too chaotic for a Christmas party.

Christmas came in the usual crush of customers, with poinsettias in red, white, and speckled pink clogging the greenhouse. I brought in my old boom box like I had the year before, and the kids and I listened to Christmas music in the office while we wrapped flowers and rang up the sales. It was one of the busiest periods of the year, and even the boss's wife left her golf course to pitch in, if bringing us minions a catered lunch can be considered helping. I don't mean to be unkind – she was a very nice lady. She just wasn't involved. Hans became scarce after the first week of December, but we hardly missed him because we were so busy.

In one of my more daring moments, I had agreed to move west with my best friend. She had recently moved to Nevada to take a lucrative media job, and she was devastatingly lonely. I felt lost without having her in the city, so I decided that I too would go west. I would be leaving my life, my friends, my job… and the old man.

Suddenly it was Christmas Eve. The day of my departure was at hand.

He didn't come to say goodbye. I wrapped a single pink rose and asked our delivery driver to drop it, along with a note, at the old man's house.

It was my last day and Gerda called the shop to wish me well. In over a year, we still hadn't met in person. "He doesn't like Christmas and hates goodbyes," she told me over the phone. Every winter his profound melancholy would overtake him, and he withdrew, surfacing only to work. He didn't socialize, didn't visit the shop, and left me to depart without a final word. I never learned why Christmas was the time of his deep depression, but I did learn not to call or send cards. One year I called on Christmas Eve, only to have Gerda tell me "No dear, he won't come to the phone." My heart ached for whatever pain he must have been feeling. But I never asked.

Despite opening up to me in so many ways, he was still so shy and guarded. Hans didn't trust anyone with his heart, least of all some kid he'd only just met in a flower shop.

When the boss locked the door at 5 o'clock, I hugged my colleagues goodbye. I'll write, I promise.

I pulled the boss aside and whispered a secret thanks for all he had done and all he had been for me. Despite the tawdry nature of our arrangement, a grudging respect and fondness existed on both sides of the equation. It was time to go. I had only two days of festivities before my cross-country train would depart. I walked away.

It was a long way from Buffalo to Reno. My friend's parents drove me as far as New York City. We left their home at 2am, her dad and I taking turns driving his minivan till we got to the city I now reside in, all these years later. I caught the west-bound train from New York, and for the next two days existed in a state of being neither here nor there. For 48 hours the train hurtled through days and nights that didn't exist, and I read to pass the time. I wrote a couple of letters. Stared out the window at the vast expanse of nothing that is the Midwest. They hid places like Nebraska and Iowa overnight, so as not to bore the passengers too much. I had a first-class ticket – a fortuitous but completely accidental purchase – so I was able to have my meals in the dining car, I had a bed to sleep in, and a shower to freshen up in. I didn't realize that these two days of non-time in non-space would be the best of my Nevada experience.

Eventually the train reached my destination. I arrived in Reno and hated it on sight. It was freezing cold, buried in snow, and ugly. I don't say that to be mean, but coming from an old, settler-inspired city like Buffalo, I was averse to the plain square buildings. Also, I had expected the warmth of the desert, as was found in Las Vegas. I hadn't done my home-work, and I was regretting it now.

For a brief moment I considered getting back on the train and taking it all the way to Los Angeles. Alas, this was the choice I had made, and I had to go through with it. Culture shock set in immediately and I pined for home. The streets were littered with vagrants – something I hadn't seen much of in my part of suburban Buffalo. In Reno they congregated near liquor stores, drunk and often belligerent to the point of being dangerous. Reno was at a much higher altitude than I was accustomed to, and I spent the first two weeks drinking massive amounts of water to stay hydrated, waiting for the nausea and dizziness of the altitude sickness to pass.

During my time in the wild west, I wrote letters. I wrote thousands of pages to my people back home, filled with gossip and tales of the extreme winter weather. My closest friends could expect two or three of the pretty lavender envelopes in their mailboxes each week. I'm sure that if I added it all up, I easily spent a month's rent on stamps in the fifteen months I lived out there. And probably another month's worth on French stationary from the fancy little boutique next to the pizza joint downtown. I took letter writing seriously, with wax and seals, which my friends back home probably never noticed, let alone appreciated.

Despite the effort I put into the letters, most of them chose to just call me instead of writing back. It was quicker, and when I announced I was leaving town, most of them signed up for cheap long distance calling plans. So much for the lost art of the letter!

Since the advent of email and texting, I have come to miss writing letters longhand. Email is free, efficient, and without soul. There's a simple pleasure that comes from using a fine pen and writing upon heavy grade paper. The catch in your throat at the last second, as you open the letterbox to drop your emotions in, saying goodbye to those words for the last time, as they will soon belong to someone else. Words on paper seem to have so much more meaning. They *last*.

Perhaps that's why I was careful about those which I actually mailed.

Some were never sent, and I began the volumes known as The Phantom Letters, from which so many of these memories have been pulled. The most honest letters, those that cried of heartbreak and loneliness, remained within those pages. They were nobody's business.

Though I was mostly single in the time I worked at the shop, I'd seen a couple of people. Besides my boss, that is. Though what we had was a big part of how we related to each other, the truth was that we had only been together a few times. One very notable rendez-vous was the day after St Valentine. I had been struggling with a serious bout of walking pneumonia in the week leading up to Valentine's, which was a Saturday that year. The boss was sympathetic when he told me, "I'm sorry, but unless you have Ebola, you *have* to come to work this week." On lucky Friday the 13th, we had one of the longest days I have ever worked. It started with receiving the roses at 6am, and ended after we had received a final shipment at 11pm. When I arrived that morning, there were two large bottles of cough syrup waiting on the counter for me. He cared.

By the time Friday was over I was exhausted, and I knew that the 14th would be just as bad, though mercifully shorter, as the doors would close at six instead of nine. Sunday the 15th would be recovery, and we'd clean the shop, which would be completely devoid of product. Everything would have sold on the 14th. The afternoon of the 15th, with me still feeling like death but no longer battling a fever, the boss approached. "I thought I'd stop by this evening." What a life.

I thought of him often, but I never wrote. It wasn't appropriate, and there was really nothing to say. We had a moment, nothing more.

Other than him and one or two other casual romances, I had had somewhat of a dalliance with my dear friend's older brother before I left home. Many of the pages I churned out were letters to him, too bare and naked and filled with longing and sadness for me to ever send. For me he had become a symbol of "home," of that life I had given up to move west, and so that pain was directed toward him. In the Phantom Letters, at least.

Some were to the old man, thanking him for all that he had given to me with his time and his words. I wrote down how I'd come to care for him in the months we spent below stairs, sharing and working. I knew that he would laugh or even become angry if I had sent him such sentimental hogwash, not to mention it might have upset Gerda. I still had not met her in person, and though she must have been aware of the old man's fondness for me, it was completely unnecessary to lead her to believe there was more to it than that. I had no desire to hurt anyone, so I kept letters like that to him unsent.

The Phantom Letters acted as a sort of diary, but one which had individual thoughts laid out for individual read-ers. Over time, five volumes of these letters were born. Three of them were from my time sequestered in the lonely wilds of Reno. Well, *wilds* may be a bit of an exaggeration. We lived three blocks from a university. Three different city buses stopped at the end of our street. But the restaurants were terrible, and people wore cowboy hats unironically.

Despite this flurry of letters, it took me months before I finally penned and sent a note to the old man. It was a card with a Monet print on the face, part of a boxed set I'd received from a friend at Christmas, just before leaving home, with the request to keep in touch. I labored over my letter to Hans for several hours, to get the light tone right. I wrote it out in the Phantom notebook first, editing and re-editing, before I finally put it in the card. Though I loved the art of letters, it felt somewhat unnatural to speak to Hans in ink, when for so long we had whispered in the cool basement. My letters to him were stilted, while trying to maintain a natural tone. Perhaps it was because I was trying to sound cheery and happy, which was alien to the pervading mood in the apartment I shared with my best friend.

Though she and I were all the other had in this western world, the grueling life was more than either of us had expected, and we withdrew into ourselves. Neither of us had much success in making other friends, I hadn't yet found a full time job, and to make matters worse, she had just lost the job that had dragged us out there. "*Not the right fit,*" they said. "*Thank you for your time,*" they said. "*Good luck in your future endeavors,*" they said. Such kind words, all of which translated to "*Sorry you're stuck in Nevada because we dragged you here!*"

When I first arrived in town, I managed to score a part-time job within four days, working at another flower shop. Fresh off my experiences in Buffalo, it was what I knew, and I looked forward to walking back into it. Alas, it just wasn't the same. It was a much less friendly atmosphere, with the owner being an aging homosexual in thrall to his elderly mother. My friend and I joked he was Norman Bates, which was funny right up until the day I discovered the body parts.

Behind the shop he had a two-story storage shed. There he kept vases, foam, body parts in jars... When I first saw the jawbone in a liquid filled jar, I figured (hoped) it was that of an animal. But animals generally don't have fillings in their molars, do they?

I soon advised him I had found an office job (I hadn't) and had to go. Many thanks and all that. I never saw him again, but I had frequent nightmares about him showing up and trying to kill me for what I'd seen. Why had I ever left Buffalo?

That left me unemployed and looking for work that didn't involve walking past the remains of potential murder victims just to grab a vase or two.

So we were stuck, penniless, hoping to just scrounge up enough cash to make the trip home. I took up drinking as a way to pass the time, which led to more and more pages in the Phantom books. She stayed in her room, hating herself for her choices and feeling guilty for making me a part of them.

I didn't really begrudge her for all that had happened. She had taken a chance on something that turned out to be a bad decision. I had made a choice to support her. We'd both get through it, somehow. But while it was all happening, one could almost see the waves of animosity and depression that gathered like smoke in the corners of our dwelling.

There were good points too, namely our bathroom. Yes,

our bathroom. We had gone to some lengths to kitsch it out with Elvis Presley décor, from the shower curtain to the swinging hips clock to the framed calendar images. There was even an Elvis Presley Boulevard street sign – purchased from Graceland, where I had visited a few years before – that took pride of place over the mirror. The finishing touches were black and "suede" blue candles and a matching blue bathmat.

The shower curtain was how my friend met her Reno boyfriend. Despite our efforts to locate an Elvis themed curtain, we were out of luck. With necessity being the mother of invention, we created a stencil of the King's silhouetted head, and headed off to an art shop (actually called Art Shoppe) downtown to get supplies. We struck up a conversation with one of the young artists who worked there on weekends.

"Hi, we need waterproof paint in velvet black and Elvis blue."

"Uh..."

"We're painting a shower curtain with Elvis heads. Here's the outline. We'll need stencil plastics and sponge brushes too."

The guy was so intrigued by the project that he showed up at our apartment that evening, after the shop (or Shoppe) had closed. The scene that greeted him was unusual. Our kitchen had been cleared of table and chairs, and we had used masking tape to put down a clear, heavy, hotel grade shower liner on the linoleum. We had used our outline and a craft knife to cut two plastic stencils – one for the black and one for the blue. We alternated the colors of acrylic paint, one black head, one blue head, and so on. We already had two rows of Elvi. My friend's new suitor was taken not only with my friend, but with our general wackiness. He crouched down and got to work next to her, taking over my "blue" duties so I could finish the spaghetti sauce that was simmering and bubbling away on the stove.

We had a fun night, all sitting around, admiring our handiwork, wolfing pasta and garlic bread and drinking wine. A new relationship was born, and more importantly, we had the coolest shower curtain anyone had ever seen. Somewhere I still have that work of art, moldering away in a storage crate. The boy, on the other hand, has long since been dispensed of.

So yes, we had our good times, but they couldn't possibly outweigh the bad ones that stemmed from fear, poverty and mutual depression.

Wherever she is today – we have since lost touch – I know my friend still shudders when she hears *Homeward Bound* in an ad or on the radio. God knows it got played often enough during my drunken nights of crying and writing. That and Dylan's *Like A Rolling Stone*. Sorry, my dearest. My epic sadness must have been hard on you, too.

One day a letter came. The script was spidery, the return address label was his. I took everything from the mailbox on my way in from a job interview for a position I neither wanted nor got: Two bills we couldn't pay, an ad for pizza we couldn't afford, and his letter. I tore the envelope open as I walked into the apartment and sat at the kitchen table with my heavy duffel coat still on.

Hallo Monica! he opened with.

News of the flower shop. He missed me. Gerda's health – she'd had a double hip replacement just before I met him and was still doing physio. All the best. Very proper, as well it should be. No substance, just as the letters I sent him had been devoid of anything meaningful. How could I tell a man who survived a war that I was unhappy because it was cold and we were broke? The truth I lived in seemed so empty compared to the truth he had lived through. I just kept it all in the Phantom Letters.

We exchanged similar nonsense on and off from Spring until the occasion of my birthday in October, when I headed home. No way was I going to waste a birthday celebration in the desolation of my western life.

I had been waitressing in a seedy casino bar on the edge of town, and finally had some cash to spend. My friend wasn't ready to deem the experience a failure yet, so we weren't moving home. I just needed a break.

The morning after I flew in, I went to have my hair done, and then drove over to the shop to see my former colleagues.

I cranked the music in my rental car, happy to be back, happy to be free of the job I was lucky to have but that I hated. But it didn't matter because I was home. Home! For the next ten days I had room to breathe, and friends to socialize with. I had sunshine, a fast car, and my hair looked fabulous.

The weather was warm and clear. I arrived at the flower shop, my hair freshly colored a lovely autumn red and blown dry. I went in through the greenhouse where, from outside, I could see they all were congregated.

They knew I was coming. I had called the boss's daughter before I left Reno, to let her know my itinerary. She said she'd let Hans know. She would be at my birthday bash that night, the day before the actual event. I had bought funky note cards with images of Elvis on them, to match the décor that my friend and I had going on in the apartment, and sent these cards out to my Buffalo friends with an invite to meet me for a birthday party. We would all be drinking and partying at a local dive bar where the drinks were cheap and the music good. Then the next day – my 22nd birthday – I would be leaving the city to go south and stay at a friend's cottage for a few days.

He sat on one of the grated metal tables he had installed himself after building the glass house for them. He was far more capable a handyman than the Greek could ever have been, with his fear of ladders (which I secretly shared) and his apparent inability to measure anything. It was hard to believe someone with such an eye for symmetry as he displayed when creating spectacular floral arrangements could be so lost when handling a measuring tape.

The bell above the door tinkled as I walked in from the bright sunshine. My emerald earrings – a gift from a lover two birthdays earlier, before I stumbled into my secret garden center world – sparkled in the light. I took my sunglasses off.

The boss's daughter saw me first and moved forward to welcome me back with a hug. But Hans spryly jumped down from the table, his movements belying his age. I flew to him. She stepped back. As far as we were concerned, there was no one else in the room. Olfactory memories are considered by science to be the strongest and most evocative. My favorite memory is the smell of him, always slightly onion-y but clean and soapy. Hat cocked on his bald pate. Long legs in patched and mended blue jeans. A long-sleeved grey sweatshirt that was so soft, I remember it to this day. He enveloped me with his lanky frame, and I clung to him. For that brief moment it was just us. I closed my eyes and he stroked my hair. The world fell away. He had pure joy at the sight of me. It was mutual.

I've occasionally wondered what the others thought in that moment as we clung to each other. Could they, in that fleeting instant, see what the two of us hid, not just from each other but from ourselves? For neither of us ever made the admission aloud. Not ever, to each other or even in our private thoughts. It was too far beyond acceptable, yet it was almost unbearably strong. He loved me: deeply, passionately and futilely. I felt the same. It was undeniable. It was as real to us as our own bones. And yet, there was never a word spoken between the old man of the earth and the young woman.

All too soon the moment passed. Life resumed. The voices of our friends made their way into our consciousness, and we broke the embrace. I said my hellos to the others and gave them comedically enhanced news from America's Biggest Little City.

Looking back over the last decade and a half, that embrace was one of the few honest experiences I've ever had in this dishonest world. I am as much a liar as all the other actors on this grand stage, so a single second of truth is precious, and worth a lifetime of lies.

I return often to that memory. His Aryan blue eyes flashing, his grin wide and sincere. The way the sun was high overhead so close to noon, and the heat inside the greenhouse. The smell of earth and peat. I search the memory to be able to once again feel his arms around me. As time passes, the ability to feel a memory fades, but still I try to recapture it.

Before I left from that birthday visit, my vacation over, returning to the emptiness of Reno, I stopped by the house and finally met Gerda for the first time. She was warm and welcoming, or at least as warm as a German could be. It was my first time in their home, and I took the proffered tea. My godfather had been East German, and I knew that to decline the hospitality of a European host was the height of insult.

Tea, cookies, and even dinner were offered and accepted. I didn't want to leave him. I didn't want to leave home. We were sitting in the little den off the kitchen. The walls and end tables were covered in photographs. There was one of Hans I especially liked. He was young – maybe his mid-forties. He still had most of his blond hair, and a thick blond mustache, in keeping with the style of the 70s. He was shirtless and tanned in a canoe. He was so handsome then. He was every bit the ideal Hitler had in mind when he began his deadly quest for the perfect race.

At one point, as I glanced around the room, my eyes landed upon a black and white photograph. In it were teenage girls, all in uniform, standing in front of a...

"My god! Is that a Nazi flag?" The words were out of my mouth before I could control them.

"That one," he gestured with one huge paw to the kitchen where Gerda was making a hearty soup for supper. "Hitler Youth." Hans shrugged. "It's what was done."

She called from the kitchen, "Did she discover I was a Nazi?"

"Ya. Looks like she might faint."

He laughed at me. To them it was funny. I was in shock.

"Monica, what did you think was happening over there for

us? We were indoctrinated, just like the Communists were. Our uniforms were better, but it was the same bullshit."

Unlike Hans, Gerda was from Germany proper, near Berlin. In the larger towns and cities, unlike out on the farms, the children were given activities and educations under the Reich. Being Hitler Youth in 1942 Germany was even more common than being a Girl Scout today.

I left their house much later than I'd expected to. As he walked me to my car, he gave me a box. It was filled with lollipops. Every one of them was cherry red.

Six months later, after the dawn of a new millennium, I had moved back home. I took a small apartment in the East End, beyond the city center. I couldn't bear the life out west and missed my friends. I missed Hans. Upon returning, I went to him. He looked relieved to have me home. We drank coffee and caught up.

Life resumed as it once was, with work, friends, clubs and parties. I started dating again, a guy that I'd seen casually before I split town. That lasted till I met my future husband the following year. I hadn't really dated the whole time I was in Reno, though I had plenty of offers while slinging drinks in a casino. It paid much better than flowers, but the mulleted drunks led to an unhealthy dislike of humanity.

There was a military base near the casino. This provided me with lots of eye candy, but nothing really came of it. One or two dinners, that was all. Not only were the soldiers better looking than the booze-soaked gamblers, but they tipped better and were a lot easier to deal with. I was in no position to be picky with work, so I kept going back night after night. The irony is that in a state where prostitution is legal, I didn't even date.

Upon returning to Buffalo, I took an apartment in the city center. I found visiting the suburbs where I grew up was getting harder and harder for me to do. The ghosts were beginning their silent creep into my reality, and I stayed away from the place I was raised. Even though I was 2500 miles closer than I was when I was in Reno, I couldn't make it all the way there. I made my friends come downtown to me. Except Hans. For him, I made the trip. Every few months I'd trek out to the burbs, and to his kitchen door.

He still drew me to him, after all that time away. I didn't see him as often as I wanted, but every now and then the draw would be so strong I couldn't sleep because of it. It would consume my thoughts all day while I toiled away in the Buffalo office of a New York law firm. I had finally given in to the corporate world and sat behind a desk all day.

Eventually I would *need* to see him and would juggle my schedule so that I could get to him. The boss's daughter knew I still kept in touch, but even she didn't know how often I journeyed to his door. I rarely if ever saw her on those pilgrimages, instead having her come into the city proper, where we could go to a club or a restaurant.

When the boss's daughter wrote me about Gerda, I had been in Brooklyn nearly six years. That's where my husband and I decided his chances were better for work when we returned from Europe. The big city! New York by proxy.

Though we had settled into new lives in Brooklyn, I was drawn back to Buffalo one last time. It was, in its way, my goodbye to the city of my birth. There would be no more happy trips back after that. My friends would never see me again – not unless they came to Brooklyn. Many of them I would cease speaking to altogether. It was a purge of the past, a resetting of my life. It wasn't easy, but without having to deal with my ghosts, I found I slept better.

When Gerda saw me on that visit, she immediately exclaimed how fat I'd gotten, much to Hans's embarrassment. It was true, though. I no longer had the muscle I'd developed from carrying bags of moist sheep manure, or trays of drinks to casino tables. My marriage was still in its infancy, and we were content. Contentment leads to girth, as I learned. Not only that, but there wasn't much to do overseas except eat and drink. It rained a lot on the North Coast of France, where we lived, so most evenings were spent in the cafés, drinking and eating. I laughed it off. We all chatted all afternoon. I never saw her again.

The truth is that I loved the old man. The truth is that fifteen years after this story first began, I love him still. Three hundred miles and a lifetime from my front door, the old man sits alone. His lover has died and left him. He waits for death to come collect his tired bones. He still haunts my dreams, though, no matter the difference in time.

I, too, sit alone. A life of adventuring, of sampling the new and exciting, cannot be done in partnership with another, and so I have been left to have my adventures by myself. Yet despite our mutual loneliness, still we remain apart.

To speak the words or to be together would be to shatter it all, causing wounds far deeper and scars more burdensome than those caused by the roses.

What we want and what we must resign ourselves to having are at odds. To touch his face and kiss his mouth would be to forfeit my life to his death. And still, there are moments when I feel the sacrifice would be worth it. To be able to cling once more to the old man, even as age and death consume us both like hellfire, would be worth it, just to have him. Then reality and common-sense break through once more, and I let the feeling go.

There is a clock that ticks incessantly at the back of my mind. Time passes. It's been seven years since I last saw Hans.

I started writing to him again after the boss's daughter told me about Gerda. Poor Hans! How terrible, after so many years. He wanted to go first. I still write to him once or twice a year, but he no longer responds. I find it sad, because he is the only person I still write to in ink.

I feel horrible that it took me till her death to start writing again after a three-year silence. When my marriage first showed signs of strain, I withdrew from a lot of people. I didn't like the idea that I'd failed, and I kept it to myself. When Gerda passed away, my husband and I were in a short-term reconciliation that was bound for a spectacular end, and I certainly didn't want to involve anyone in the madness I was enduring. But I had to let him know I cared.

In addition to the letters I send him, there are still those I keep for myself. The Phantom Letters. The love letters that can never be sent.

I know I'm running out of time to say goodbye. I must go home and battle the ghostly sentries of my past to reach his side.

2

Return

"...ten minutes from our stop in Buffalo." I awoke on the highway just outside of town to the sound of the driver announcing my stop. I blinked a few times. Sleeping in my contact lenses always made them gummy. Thankfully I had solution in my bag, which should help.

Buffalo. A return to my demons and ghosts. I traveled in the dead of night and arrived just after dawn. It was my intention to tend to the business at hand and return to my dogs by midnight.

The overnight coach dropped me not 200 yards from where the old man first offered me candy. I popped into the donut shop in the strip mall to use the bathroom and freshen up before I went to him. It had been a cramped night on the bus, and I looked a fright. I brushed my hair out and re-arranged the clips that held it back from my face. Cleaned the sleep out of my eyes and applied mascara. Brushed the fur off my teeth and put on a coat of demure pink lipstick.

Back outside, I looked over at the still-sleeping flower shop perched on the corner, its neon signage bright against the dawn sky. This was where it all began, and I took a moment to embrace the memories. Then I turned away and headed north toward the lake.

I could have hailed a cab or caught a city bus. I could have rented a car. Instead, I chose to gather my thoughts and purify myself by walking the three miles to his house. My legs needed stretching anyway, after being cooped up on the bus for six hours. By the time I arrived, I knew, he would be awake and pottering about in his garden.

Suburbia. The place that had – for good or ill – created me. I came pre-equipped with all the usual Generation X suburban idiosyncrasies: an affection for sleeping pills and a tendency to drink alone, the desire to bed a buffet's worth of married men, and a predisposition to divorce, as I had two years earlier. That's how the latchkey generation was raised, and that's how we remained. Reality Bites, they told us. Indeed.

My marriage was fine right up until it wasn't. It went from happy to all of a sudden, we had absolutely no interest in one another. Our lives became separate, and I took a lover. Or two. We both did, before finally deciding it would be a good idea to take a break, and each got our own places. But since goodbyes are rarely final, we ended up back together, caught up in a destructive death spiral that almost cost me my life. Despite it all, I still missed him from time to time.

On my feet I wore comfortable and practical sneakers, incongruous with the trim black suit I sported. In my shoulder bag I kept the feminine heels I'd change into nearer the house. One of the idiosyncrasies of the suburbs is that a person walking down the street is immediately noticed. They are different, like the one real human left at the end of Invasion of the Body Snatchers. *Everyone* drives in the suburbs. It was one of the reasons I stayed downtown so long – I felt so exposed when I headed to the burbs. In the downtown core, and in a city like Brooklyn, pedestrians were the norm. I forgot how naked I could feel. Thankfully it was too early for most of the suburbanites to be up and moving about. I had the place to myself.

The morning air was chilly. Mid-October. Same time of year, but a lifetime away from my birthday visit. I wished I'd brought a coat or shawl, but I knew his kitchen would be warm and inviting as always. Even without Gerda there.

It was hard to reconcile the happy girl who visited for her 22nd birthday with the fearful woman who had to battle her demons just to be there.

Over the years between marriage and divorce, the ghosts of the past caught up with me. All the bodies buried in Buffalo – both real and figurative – kept me from returning. Where once I was trapped out in the wilds of northern Nevada and pined for home, I now avoided it lest it consume me. Homesickness was now totally alien to me. I was completely without a home, especially since my divorce.

I did return once, just once, without seeing the old man. My best childhood friend had called to say her grandmother had passed away. I was very close to the family and to Nanny and returned for the funeral. Huge mistake. I once again trod over the soil of the cemetery where my own parents rested in perpetuity, and became overwhelmed with sadness and panic. Was death all my home had to offer me? Though I had intended to visit with the Hans and Gerda that afternoon, once the funeral activities were over, I instead fled and took an earlier train back to the Megopolis I now referred to hollowly as "home." I was in Buffalo for fewer than 20 hours.

Yet here I was, returning at last, to say goodbye to another old friend, this time before death could claim him. Damned death. It owned my past. And I was only here to race it to my dear friend. I refused to let it own him too, before I had a chance to say the things I needed to say.

As I moved away from the shopping corridor where the coach left me and into the sleepy lakeside heart of suburbia, I thought of how quiet it all was. My apartment in Brooklyn was on a major thoroughfare, with traffic and sirens screaming by at all hours. I was enjoying the silence. The lakeshore to Hans's was somehow insulated, like after a snowstorm – the birds and occasional cars had no echo.

In addition to the body count, Buffalo was also stacked with broken hearts, failed romances, and friendships turned sour. It was where I met my ex-husband. It was where I sold my flesh. I walked along the lakeshore toward Hans, and I could feel the specters of my past creeping up behind me, ready to swallow me alive. Knowing I could never out-run them, I nonetheless picked up the pace. Now Gerda was among the dead, and it was too late to say goodbye to her. While that saddened me, I knew that it was not any allegiance to her that brought me here this day. I was here for him.

As the sky brightened and the sun broke through, I changed my shoes, smoothed my hair again, and approached the house, coy behind its trimmed hedges. Unlike the shoe-maker's barefooted children, this landscaper's house and land were perfectly groomed. Bypassing the front door entirely, I went round the side. Only strangers entered by the front door. The rest of us went by way of the kitchen.

He wasn't out in the garden as I'd expected, but I was heartened to see that it was as lush as it had been when last I visited. In addition to the cedar saplings he grew for his customers' lawns, Hans had pumpkins and other squash just ready for harvest. I could see the dying tomato plants from the summer months – soon he would yank these out for composting.

His two Chevy trucks were parked in front of the free-standing garage out back, next to the garden. His tan summer truck, for hauling, and the old beat-up red winter one, with the plow on the front. I was amazed that they were both still running after all these years. Then again, I was also amazed that Hans was still chugging along. In the garage, under the tarp, was Gerda's baby. She had had a late 70s model Corvette that she drove everywhere, at least till her hips went out and she couldn't get in and out of the low seats. While Hans was out raking and plowing his fortunes, Gerda worked her whole life as a pharmaceutical chemist, and retired with a hefty pension. Being childless, she liked to spend her money on nice things for herself, and why not? It was such a difference though from Hans, who wore the same tattered rags year after year. Gerda liked to travel, but would go on vacation alone, because Hans was a homebody. They had been a very odd couple, but they had lasted right up to the end. Better than I could say.

I wondered if he ever took that sleek baby out for a spin. I think she'd want him to.

The old man had no idea I was coming. The last letter I'd sent had been months earlier, and though it intimated I may come calling, there was no time or date set. Nor did I call the boss's daughter to let her know. I wouldn't even be seeing her – my trip was a straight in-and-out mission, as precise as a military operation. Like a ninja, I would travel both ways in darkness, avoiding as many eyes as I could.

A few people in Brooklyn twigged in the past few months that I might be heading homeward, but they knew neither when nor why. Certainly not why. This was my secret. I'd never told a soul in my daily life about the old man, and even if I had, no one would understand. Even I didn't understand what brought me back. All my Brooklyn friends knew was that there was something I needed to take care of, something time sensitive, and that I had to get to it soon. It was clear over the months that I was becoming agitated about something from "home," but I wouldn't go into specifics. How could I tell a group of hip 30- and 40-somethings – friends and colleagues from the big city – that I needed to go home to tell an elderly non-relative that I loved him before he died? He wasn't a parent or grandparent. In truth, he hadn't even been in my life all that long. Only a year, really. But he'd been in my heart for fifteen.

I should have been home sooner. I had tried. I had tried and failed again and again to fight the demons. My email inbox was peppered with unused ticket confirmations, almost a dozen of them. Hundreds of dollars in non-refundable coach tickets proved that I had great intentions, but not nearly enough bravery to make it back. I chickened out every time. Once I made it as far as Binghamton – the halfway point – before rushing off the bus and waiting for a return coach to Brooklyn. I was a coward.

It was unreal that I could be so drawn and so repelled at the same time, like a magnet that kept spinning positive and negative toward its partner. Getting to the old man's door was like walking through Hell to find him. But at last, I had arrived.

Even this successful journey required a small handful of Valium when I got on the bus at midnight. I knew I had to sleep my way home; I couldn't face it with my eyes open. Though still drowsy, I had a chemically induced measure of calm I wouldn't have otherwise had.

I didn't just have to battle the past or say goodbye. There was another truth I'd come to share, a truth whose time had come. A reckoning was to be had this sunny autumn morning, and I feared that it would not only alter the future, but it also ran the risk of erasing a beautiful part of my past.

Valium or no valium, I hesitated as I reached for the kitchen door. My heart was pounding. I took deep breaths until I built up the courage to go in. I didn't knock. I simply tried the door, and it gave way as it always had.

And there, at the old Formica table, steaming coffee and newspaper in hand, bifocals perched on his nose, sat the old man to whom my heart was drawn from a distance and a lifetime away. He hadn't changed much. A few more wrinkles and the bifocals were new. He still wore jeans with patches sewn in for mending and a long-sleeved undershirt with a tee on top. His felt hat was on the table, a Bavarian peaked cap with a feather.

I took all this in only incidentally. I didn't take my eyes off him.

He looked up at the interloper who had wandered into his kitchen. "What are you…" He put his coffee down.

"Candyman."

He stood, recognition on his face. "Monica."

I watched conflicting emotions cross his face as I put my bag down and took the two steps toward his arms. Confusion, followed by understanding and finally peace. And in a split second I was there, my face pressed against his chest, still broad and firm despite his age. His arms wrapped round me tightly, as if fearing I was merely a mirage that might at any moment fade.

"Monica… Where have you been?" He muttered into my hair. "You've been gone so long."

"It doesn't matter," I said with tears choking my words. "I'm here now."

He stroked my hair. "Don't cry." Yet when I looked up there were tears in the weathered creases of his own face.

I touched his cheek and traced the path of a tear down to the lines around his mouth.

"What are you doing here?"

"You never answered my letters. So I mailed myself – overnight express. Now you *have* to answer!"

He smiled, and his eyes lit up. I took it as my opportunity.

There was something I had come to do. Something I would never again have the chance for. With a deep, desperate breath, I stretched on my heels and pressed my lips to his. It didn't matter how mad it was to do this, or how apocalyptic the fallout might be. I only had the one chance.

He drew back, eyes wide with surprise, though his arms remained loosely around my waist, his hands at my hips.

"Moni-"

I silenced his shock once more with my mouth. For a second he tensed, struggling within himself, common sense trying hard to conquer the insanity of the moment, and then finally resigned, his lips softening into mine. A culmination of fifteen years in that kiss.

His arms tightened around me. His kiss deepened and my head spun. I, too, fought the rising tide of common sense that threatened to shatter the moment, in order to hold fast to this one mad kiss.

His sanity kicked in first and he broke the spell, pushing

me away by my shoulders and holding me at arm's length lest I tempt him again. He looked hurt.

"Why did you come here?"

I took a moment to recover my thoughts. I closed my eyes and tried to steady myself. One beat, two. Too many.

"Why did you come here?" His voice was rising in anger.

Anger? I opened my eyes.

"Is it money?" He asked. There was rage in his face.

"Money?" I was confused. The pounding heart, spinning head and general grogginess with which I came armed to this meeting muddled me. "You think I traveled all night because I want... money?" I was disgusted, having him of all people think I would have traded my kiss for his money.

"How much do you need?" He reached back for his wallet.

I put my hands up as if to defend myself from a physical blow, which is how this felt. I shook my head. "Not you. Never you. You misunderstand." I took a step back, my eyes wide with horror.

He knew! He must have known. The boss must have gossiped about our arrangement. My beloved Hans knew I was a whore. I was devastated. How had he learned it? What had the boss said? After all those years, why would he break the confidence that would hurt him more than me? Though looking at the angry Hans now, I wondered if in fact it hadn't hurt me more.

"Misunderstand? You show up out of the blue and you, you..." He couldn't bring himself to say the words. He looked nauseous at the mere sight of me, this lowly creature of lust and greed.

"I kissed you," I said quietly.

"Why, if not for my money?"

I could only imagine what the boss had said. An easy piece, in the vernacular of his generation. For so long I had hidden parts of my life from the old man, lest he know how truly worthless I was. Worthless. Unworthy. Unworthy of his stories and his confidences.

After the boss there had been others, some one-off, some concurrent. Some unusual in their proclivities, and in this area I excelled. The negotiated rate was higher, and I used the given opportunity to work out all the anger and hatred I had in my heart. Never could I let the old man know the things I had done to these faceless men in exchange for their money. What they requested of me was to be degraded and humiliated, which in turn left some of that degradation etched on me. But they paid the bills.

Never could I allow him to think I saw him merely as one of my marks.

A decade earlier, after I had returned from the wilds of Reno, I lived right in town, as far away from the suburbs as I could get and still be in the same city. I visited him and Gerda on a Saturday afternoon, taking the bus all the way out. A two-hour trip. He offered to drive me home. I asked instead if he would mind driving a bit further west and out to where my cousin lived. He dropped me at her door with a hug and a kiss on the cheek.

Months later I visited him again. I would try to make the pilgrimage once per quarter, at least. He had the paper open, and conversationally mentioned that the son of a Hungarian man he had known when he first came over had been arrested for running a prostitution ring. Before I knew it, the words were out of my mouth "That's my cousin's husband!" He frowned. My worlds were too close to colliding. He had delivered me to the door of a common bawdy house, and he knew it. We never spoke of it again.

And now, so many years later, those worlds were once more colliding as he hurled his accusation at me. When cornered, attack.

"I never wanted your money, you stupid old fool!" My own voice was becoming louder. "And if I did, I would have had it a long time ago." My eyes narrowed as I plunged the final dagger in. "I assure you old man, you would have been more than glad to hand it over." I spat these last words at him.

It hurt so much, because everything I ever wanted from him, he had already freely given me. None of it was money. I only ever wanted his time.

Tears of anger and shame streamed down my face.

"Then why did you come?"

"Because you're going to die." My anger deflated in the harshness of reality.

"What?"

"Because you are the better part of a century old Hans, and I wasn't going to let you go without telling you."

"Telling me what?"

I hesitated. Took a deep breath. "That I've loved you for as long as I've known you. I just wanted you to know that you've been with me every day for fifteen years and you'll be with me always. I wanted to say thank you for all you've been for me. For sharing your past with me. For allowing me into your life. For your kindness. I just wanted to say… goodbye."

I turned away, reaching for the kitchen door. As I opened

it, I looked back. The old man was crying. He hung his head and cried. Now it was he who was ashamed.

"Monica," he sobbed.

"That's not my name. Clearly you have me confused with that girl. I might have been her once, but not anymore."

He raised his head to look at me. "No. You never were."

He took me by the wrist and pulled me back till I stood once more before him. He studied my face, searching for any proof of deception. There was none. I was standing there exposed, with my heart ripped to shreds. I had held it out to him, and he had torn it to pieces. The kindly old man had fiercely turned on me. Yet I had come all this way, and I didn't want to give up till he understood what I was telling him.

"I shouldn't have come. I'm sorry. I just needed you to know before... before it's too late."

My face was burning with shame. I tried to pull away, tried to leave, but his grip on my wrist was so tight it was painful.

He kissed me. Hard and brutally. I tasted blood; his or mine, I didn't know. I turned my head and gasped. "What are you doing?" I cried.

"Looking for your lies." And he kissed me again, devouring me like a savage. He wanted to hurt me, and he did.

I couldn't fight him and I didn't want to. I gave myself over to his anger and his insecurity. The world stopped just as it had on that day so many years before, in the warmth of the greenhouse.

On and on we kissed, till I was breathless and he was convinced. I wasn't lying. I was sincere. I still held out the shredded heart, beating and bleeding in my hands, and he accepted it. At last, he accepted it.

"I'm sorry. I'm so sorry. I never thought..."

He didn't know! My secret was safe, and Hans continued to live in blissful ignorance of my misdeeds. The boss had kept our dirty secret. Relief flooded me. Relief, and something else.

"And how could you know? I've been gone almost ten years. I'm surprised you even remembered me."

"How could I forget you? I still have the letters you sent. I just... what could I say?" His forearms rested on my shoulders; his forehead pressed against mine. "Forgive me?"

"There's nothing to forgive!" I was happy, elated even. I wrapped my arms around his waist tightly, and leaned again into his chest. I was safe there. I was forgiven. "I can only imagine... This totally isn't how you planned to spend your day, is it?"

He laughed, let me go and pulled out a chair at the table for me. "Coffee?" I nodded. "No, I was going to rake leaves today. This is a huge improvement. Sugar?"

"Just milk, please."

He put a steaming cup before me and sat back down where, only a few minutes before, he had been having a perfectly normal morning.

He studied me for a moment. I did the same. He was summing up all the ways I had changed and how the world had aged me since he'd last seen me. My face was still mostly without lines, and any grey in my hair was camouflaged. But my eyes... my eyes were tired. I'd seen too much and done too much in the years I'd been away. I'd lost everything and started over when my marriage collapsed. I'd starved and struggled and even been homeless for a spell, but that too I wanted to keep to myself. My eyes were closer to those of Monica than they had ever been.

While I wasn't averse to letting Hans know a little of what life had been like, I saw no cause to concern him over things that were done and put forever away. I was now finally thriving and trying to catch up with myself. I had a great job, a nice apartment I could afford, and hobbies like marathon running and hiking mountains. I had traveled the world. These were the kind of things my letters contained.

The same way he asked what he could possibly say to me in letters was how I too had felt writing to him. It wasn't so much the content, as I just wanted him to know I was thinking of him. I left the darker details out.

Where Hans was concerned, I simply wanted to be the good little girl I had never actually been capable of being. I wanted to be whatever I saw in his eyes when he looked at me, and if that meant hiding some painful truths, so be it.

Perhaps it was an occupational hazard, but I was something different to each person who knew me. The trusted confidante. The bossy dominatrix. The sultry whore. The passionate lover. And the little child. With Hans I wanted to be both honest and yet deceive him, in that he could never know of my other personae.

All these little boxes of my personality were arranged and rearranged as the occasion called for, and I sometimes wondered if there was a real me. Were they all me, or were they all false? Was there anyone out there, myself included, who had access to all the facets at once? Perhaps my parents might have, but that was so long ago. My husband had seen several of them, and it proved too much. Too much for one person to bear, as if my collection of personalities were some Pandora's Box that once opened, could never be closed. All the sorrows of the world existed when you put all my facets together and built a complete me. It was better in many ways for me to keep all my personae carefully apart.

Hiding parts of me from Hans was neither honest nor dishonest. It was simply the way I presented myself to everyone, as needed. I was everything to everyone. And nothing to myself.

"So. Why now?"

I let out a long sigh. Good question. How to explain the ticking clock?

"I've been trying to come here for… months. I just needed to see you, and I've been fighting with myself about it. My last letter… I tried to explain what it felt like to come home. It must have sounded like gibberish to you, but it's not easy for me to be here."

"No, I understood. Remember, I've only been back twice in all the years I've lived here. I know about pain and ghosts and putting the past behind you."

Of course he did. He lived with his pain every day, and more so every Christmas. I asked him once, long ago, if he ever visited Austria. He'd told me that Gerda had gone over pretty often, but that he'd only gone over to bury his mother and one other doomed vacation to Germany and Austria that Gerda had prodded him into. He hated looking back. It's not the *looking* back that hurt me, though. It was the literal feeling stepping back into the past. From 300 miles away, I could think of Buffalo and remember the good times. From the belly of the beast, I saw only the pain. I saw only the death and the tears.

"I meant it, Hans. There isn't a lot of time. I've lost so many people who were important to me. I just couldn't bear to lose you too."

"You coming here can't stop death, you know."

No kidding. "I know. But I could at least see your face one last time, thank you for all you've given me – all you've been to me – and then, if I don't come back again…" I trailed off. "It's so hard to come back. I'm not sure we'll see each other again. I would never forgive myself if I didn't get back here in time. How old *are* you, Hans?" No one knew. It was another of his closely guarded secrets.

"Ha! You know better than to ask that!" Thwarted again. I might never learn his age. At least not till his year of birth was etched on a tombstone.

"Why did you, uh…" He cast his eyes down. After all these years, they were still a brilliant blue, unclouded by age. Despite the rheuminess and the pockets of flesh beneath them, they were still so beautiful and bright. The room seemed a little chillier when he took them off my face, as if the sun had gone behind a cloud.

I'd never known a grown man so shy.

"Kiss you?" Twice now he'd been unable to say the words. "I wanted to." It was the simplest truth. "I've wanted to for a long time, but it never seemed like the right thing to do. It still doesn't but... At least the timing is better. I don't know why, Hans. I don't know why I needed to, but it's why I'm here. It's why I got on a bus at midnight and came to your door. It's why... It's why I've been writing to you every few months. I've felt this way for a long time, and kept it to my-self. I got on with my life, and you got on with yours, with Gerda. But now I hear this clock ticking incessantly..." I was unsure about telling him about the clock, but I had to. At this point, there was nothing to lose. "There's a clock, and for months I've been hearing it. Go back, go back, go back... Go to him. And I've been fighting it. I've wanted to come, but just couldn't bring myself to do it. But now I'm here. I'm here and I kissed you. I didn't come here for a visit, no one else is going to see me. The boss's daughter doesn't know I'm here. Hell, I don't even know if my uncle across town is still alive, and I won't be finding out today. I came here for you, and I'll be back in my bed by midnight. Here and gone before the rest of my demons even know I arrived."

"When you were born, I was older than you are now."

"Yeah, I know." I felt like I was being scolded, and like a scolded child, I shrugged. "So?"

"So kissing me is like kissing your grandfather."

"No, that was different."

He looked alarmed.

"Just kidding! Thought we could use some comic relief. So you're old. I covered that with the whole 'dying any minute now' thing, didn't I?"

"You're a fool." But his eyes were laughing. They were on me once more, and I was warm.

"Guilty as charged. Only a fool would travel all night just to ruin your breakfast."

"You didn't. You made my day, actually. You look wonderful, as beautiful as always. I'm just... surprised. I can't even believe you're here. It's been a few months since your last letter, so I expected another one soon, but I never expected you at my door. I'm glad you're here. Forget everything else."

"Everything else, as you put it, is *why* I'm here." I reached across the table and put my small white hand over his big weathered one. His skin jumped a bit, as if I'd shocked him, but he relaxed. Turned his hand over and took mine. Studied it, as if it held the answers. "Hans, do you want me to go? I didn't come here to upset you or confuse you. I did what I came here to do. I said what I needed to say." I meant it. There was nothing left to be done. I could take an earlier bus back to Brooklyn, get back to my dogs sooner. Get away from this godforsaken suburb before the Valium completely wore off. I could do all these things, but I just didn't want to. I didn't want to pull my hand away, or get up to leave. I didn't want to walk away for what I knew would be the last time.

"Don't." He squeezed my hand. "Stay. Stay because of... everything else."

His eyes silently asked a question, and my face with love and longing written across it silently answered.

Hans didn't work that day. No leaves were raked in the October sunshine. I did not make it back to Brooklyn before midnight. He stayed home, and at the end of a fifteen year wait, my old vagabond made love to me. He was tender and so strong. His body, though old, was well cared for and took to mine with the passion of a much younger man.

He led me through the house and up the stairs to the room he had shared with Gerda for so many years. To their bed. But Gerda was dead and Hans was dying and I was alive. I was alive and I would give a little of my life to him.

The house itself was dead, too, trapped in a time warp. Decorated in the 1970's and kept in picture-perfect stasis. Pale blue plush wall-to-wall up the stairs to the bathroom where the shaggy tank and lid cozies remained. To the left was the bedroom, with dusty rose ruffled bedspread and yellowed plastic on the lampshades. It was possible that the house had remained untouched since before I was born.

I stood in the doorway of the bedroom, needing to be invited in.

He took my hand and pulled me to him. "Are you sure?"

He feared my rejection as I feared his.

"So many years, Hans... Of course I'm sure." One chance. That's all I could think of. I knew how crazy this was, how it broke the unspoken rules we'd adhered to for so long, but one chance, one chance... We only ever have one chance.

My desire was strong, but I was nervous. I was thirty-five, and he was fifty years my senior. So many what-ifs. So much unknown. His body... what would it be like? Would it respond? Would I shy away?

I wondered what it would have been like to be with him in his prime, when his body was hard and strong. Or even fifteen years before, when we met in the cool caves below the shop.

The boss had tried to take me there once, and I rebuked him. "I'll pay you," he whispered, putting his hand inside my blouse.

"You may not give a damn about your daughter, but I do, and she's barely twenty feet away," I hissed. "Now get off me!"

He recognized his foolishness and left me to get on with my work. Of course, an appointment for later was set.

What if it had been Hans? What if he had been the one to touch me in the dark corner under the stairs?

He unbuttoned the fitted jacket of my suit. I let it fall away and shivered as the air hit the ivory silk of the camisole beneath. I reached behind my back and undid my skirt, letting that drop, too. I stood before my old gypsy in nothing but a chemise and panties. His jaw clenched. When was the last time he saw a younger woman undressed? When he himself was in his thirties? Forties? Was I even born the last time he was with a younger woman?

Though he never named names, and kept the gory details to himself, he had confessed various affairs he'd had over the years he'd been with Gerda. Upstairs the Greek and the boss gossiped. There were rumors of the who and the when, and the list included some very old, very moneyed family names. Sigh. They always went for the gardener, didn't they? It was such a cliché.

"Hans?"

"I'm..."

"Nervous?"

He nodded.

"Me too." I leaned in, pressed my lips to his. Instinctively he put his hands on me, and their coarseness on my bare arms shocked me. My nipples hardened.

I lifted the bottom of his shirts and placed my hands flat against the skin beneath. I dug the tips of my fingers into the hair on his chest.

"Take them off," I whispered.

"I'm afraid." We had the same fears.

"I want to touch you." They were words I had used years before on other nervous men, men who feared rejection though they paid handsomely for unconditional acceptance. Men like my boss. But unlike those men, I truly did want to touch Hans.

He removed his shirts and stood bare-chested before me. I smiled, not only for his reassurance, but in relief. Hans's body was fit and firm from years of hard work. Work had toned the muscles of his arms and torso. Sure, the skin was loose, and the hair on his chest was the gray of a ship's hull, but he was still beautiful.

I nearly reached for his belt, wanting to undo it, but I held back. Hans was of another era, where men took charge in the bedroom and forward women were whores. He had already made that accusation to me that morning. I didn't want to compound it.

No matter how mutual a feeling is, women are obliged to play certain roles the first time to bed with a man. Virgin or whore. The role I needed to play that day was demure. I no longer fit in either of the categories. I was a middle-aged divorcée. I stood in the bedroom of a man old enough to have sired my mother. Only demure would do. We both knew there was something inherently unnatural about what was happening, but neither of us wanted to put a stop to it. I cast my eyes down and waited. It was his move.

He brushed his fingers across my right shoulder, slipping the ribbon of strap down, where it hung carelessly against my upper arm. He did the same thing to the left, and the silk garment dropped to my waist.

The idea of what was about to take place had been with me almost since the beginning. I awoke one morning after a dream, and instead of feeling repulsed by the images my sleeping mind had created, I was captivated by them. It wasn't long after my birthday visit home, and our epic embrace had already told me that my bond with him went beyond cleaning roses. I knew I could never mention these thoughts aloud, never even add them to my Phantom Letters, but from time to time I would relax the control I had over them and let them come.

Over the intervening years, I occasionally allowed my mind to travel to that secret place. It was perhaps what drew me back to his door again and again, regardless of my romantic or domestic situation. Because the secret was mine alone, it never affected those I was with. It never tarnished my marriage, or touched Gerda, or even Hans. But it was powerful, and it was what continued to put ink on paper and stamps on letters.

He sat down on the edge of the bed, and drew me to him. He put his hands on my waist, pushing the camisole and my panties down over my hips. At last I was completely naked, though his jeans remained resolutely in place.

I climbed onto the bed, a knee on either side of him, suspending myself above him, my hands on his shoulders. His arms went round me, and he allowed himself to fall back, pulling me with him. Rolling on top of me, he kissed me. His rough hands traveled over my body, scratching me, scorching me. He took his time, exploring every inch of me. Though I was now middle-aged, to him I was fresh and young. My skin was elastic, it was smooth. My breasts were still high and round. I'd had no children, and gravity had thus far been kind to me.

Back when I was 20, my boss had groaned against my belly, happy he said to touch young flesh. Though his wife was a beautiful woman, nothing could compare to the elasticity of the young, I suppose.

The past few years since my divorce had been about self-improvement, and that meant shedding the pounds, running half-marathons, and generally keeping fit. I had even done a 6-month stint on a Kansas farm, hoisting hay bales and working out in the sun. It reminded me of those days of tagging the roses and working through the summer months outside at the garden center. I was fit and strong, and Hans was able to appreciate the benefit of my young, firm body.

His lips traveled between my breasts in a line down past my navel. He kissed the insides of my thighs. He moved toward my center, his mouth hungry. My breath caught in my throat. My body cried out for the loving abuses of those rough hands. My most sensitive place was being assaulted by calluses, but his touch was so gentle.

At last, breathless, I heard him loosening his belt. Against my will I froze. This was it, the moment was upon me, and like all things in life that overwhelmed me, I sought to run from it. I racked my brain, trying to remember how long it had been since I was shy and afraid in bed with a man. I came up empty. Sex was never something I'd been afraid of, and was instead a tool I used often as a weapon. A means to an end. Yet in that bed where the ghost of Gerda remained, I was shy and scared. I was like a child.

He looked at me, his own hesitation written plain across his face. What was about to be done could never be undone. Yet every cell of me screamed out for this. It was part of the natural progression, a destination to which we'd both been headed for almost half my life.

We cast aside our fears. Taking in the reality of his abilities versus mine, I maneuvered him onto his back and climbed astride him. The roles fell away – virgin and whore blurred at this point, and in less than a heartbeat we were fused. All the fear and uncertainty melted away. I gave myself to it. To him. I was shocked at the force with which his strong hands gripped my hips and led me, and shocked by his stamina. Whatever expectations I may have had were far surpassed by the reality. Whatever fears I had were unfounded.

Throughout the afternoon our tangled sweaty bodies owned each other. Sometimes I cried from both joy and from a sense of imminent loss. Sometimes the tears were his. I traded my life for his death, taking and giving.

Monica and the Candyman: two misfit souls making a last stand, together.

I wasn't back in Brooklyn in time for supper. As the sky turned to purple twilight, the old gypsy and I found a measure of peace, dozing in each other's arms.

3

Goodbye

"...ten minutes from our stop in Buffalo." I awoke on the highway just outside of town to the sound of the driver announcing my stop. I blinked a few times. Sleeping in my contact lenses always made them gummy. Thankfully I had solution in my bag, which should help.

Buffalo. A return to my demons and ghosts. I traveled in the dead of night and arrived just after dawn. It was my intention to tend to the business at hand and return to my dogs by midnight.

The overnight bus dropped me not 200 yards from where the old man first offered me candy. I popped into the donut shop in the strip mall to use the bathroom and freshen up before I went to them. It had been a cramped night on the bus, and I looked a fright. I brushed my hair out and re-arranged the clips that held it back from my face. Cleaned the sleep out of my eyes and applied mascara. Brushed the fur off my teeth.

I looked over at the flower shop perched on the corner, its neon signage bright against the dawn sky. This was where it all began.

I walked across the long strip-mall parking lot toward it. Though it was barely six in the morning, there were four cars in the driveway already.

Suburbia. The place that had – for good or ill – created me. I came pre-equipped with all the usual Generation X suburban idiosyncrasies: an affection for sleeping pills and a tendency to drink alone, the desire to bed a buffet's worth of married men, and a predisposition to divorce, as I had two years earlier. That's how the latchkey generation was raised, and that's how we remained. Reality Bites, they told us. Indeed.

My marriage was fine right up until it wasn't. It went from happy to all of a sudden, we had absolutely no interest in one another. We both did, before finally deciding it would be a good idea to take a break, and each got our own places. But since goodbyes are rarely final, we ended up back together, caught up in a destructive death spiral that almost cost me my life. Despite it all, I still missed him from time to time.

On my feet I wore comfortable and practical sneakers,

incongruous with the trim black suit I sported. In my shoulder bag I kept the feminine heels I'd change into later that day.

The morning air was chilly. Mid-October. Same time of year, but a lifetime away from my birthday visit. I wished I'd brought a coat or shawl, but I knew the store would be warm and inviting as always. Even without Hans.

I knocked on the locked front door. Allyson soon appeared, coming up the stairs from the basement. The basement I spent so many hours in with the old man. She unlocked the door and let me in. She hadn't changed much in fifteen years. I wondered if she thought the same of me.

"You made it!" She said, giving me a quick hug. "We're all downstairs."

I followed her in, taking in the many changes that the shop had undergone over the years. It was bigger, airier. There was fresh paint in pale blue. It looked wonderful, but still had the same feeling of family and comfort.

"You're just in time – the flowers just came."

As I touched down on the bottom step, I entered my past. They all stood around the two tack tables – Leo, my boss, now retired; Nick, the chain-smoking Greek manager, also retired; Allyson, who now ran the shop; Mark, her brother. Only one man was missing.

I chucked my bag under the stairs, removed my jacket, and approached the tables in just my camisole.

"How many times have I told you I hate it when you work in a tank top?" Leo bellowed as he came over to hug me.

I smiled. "You can fire me at the end of the day."

To Nick, from whom I had always received my orders, "Where do I start?"

He gestured to the open box on the floor. Roses. Red roses.

As though fifteen years hadn't passed, I picked up a bundle wrapped in corrugated cardboard to protect the heads.

"Here." Mark handed me a rake. I took up a spot at the table he and his father were working at. Only very early in the mornings on Valentine's Day and Mother's Day saw us all below stairs, working together.

The retired men moved slower now, but the tearing and cutting was still second nature to them. Muscle memory. I soon found my rhythm too, pulling the rake through the leaves. It was harder than I remembered. It was harder than typing in an office all day. I moved as slowly as the retirees.

"Clean them all the way up," Nick instructed. After all,

they weren't going back in the fridges for sale. "I need them stripped."

I tightened my grip around the protective cardboard and went high with the rake. A shower of leaves and thorns sprayed out over the table and floor.

The three crates from Bogotá quickly emptied. All the white roses were done, and only a few bundles of red remained.

"Finish up here," Nick said to Mark and me. "Allyson and I will start setting up."

Allyson was cleaning the other table of leaves and stems, and setting out the soaking blocks of green floral foam from which the arrangements would be formed.

There was no small-talk down there in the dark as the sun rose on the world above. Each of us was wrapped in his or her own thoughts. I was deep in my memories, of all the hours spent down here, alone or with Hans.

Leo went upstairs to put the notice on the door. The shop would not be open today. Unprecedented. That little flower shop was open every day except Christmas Day.

I grabbed my last bundle of twenty red roses, and as I pulled the rake through, I yelped in pain. A thorn had caught me on the wrist bone, tearing a gash and drawing blood.

Mark smiled. "Welcome back."

I worked through the pain as I had always done. Soon the cut would be gummed up with the sap from the stems, anyway. The blood of the roses.

When the bundle was stripped and clipped, I let it loose from the cardboard.

Nineteen red roses tumbled free. Nineteen red, and one rare, precious black.

"Oh look!" I cried, picking up the unusual bloom. The others looked. Even after so many years and the millions of roses that came and went through the shop, a black rose was still an occasion to stop and stare.

"You know the rules: You found it, you keep it," Nick said, lighting another cigarette.

"I'll take it with me," I said, clipping the bottom and putting a water tube on it. I set it aside for later.

Nick and Allyson were the artists among us, so when Mark and I were finished we cleaned up and went upstairs to sit with Leo. Sit and wait for the masterpieces to be brought up. I took my black rose up to show him.

While we'd been downstairs he'd popped out to fetch us coffee.

"Here," he handed me a cup. It smelled good, steam rising in the semi-darkness. I needed it after the long night on the bus, and the handful of Valium it had required to give me the courage to come back home.

I held out my rose like a small child proffering a dandelion. "Look."

"We haven't had one of those in years. Maybe ten years! Well done."

Mark took his coffee and went out to the greenhouse to water the plants. With one exception, this day was just like any other at the shop.

Leo and I made small talk while we waited for Nick and Allyson to come up.

"You cut yourself," he gestured to my right wrist.

"Somehow seems appropriate that I should bleed today." I took a sip of coffee, now cool enough to drink. "How've you been?"

"Getting old. Doing the usual, golf, chasing young women."

I nodded. That was Leo.

"You look good."

I laughed. "Don't get any ideas, old man!"

"Too late!"

"You haven't changed a bit."

"Hell no. Young at heart." He paused, took a sip. Looked at me. "Why'd you stay away so long?"

I didn't know how to answer. How could I sum up years of absence, years of fear, in a few words over coffee? How could I tell him that it simply hurt too much to come home?

"He asked for you, you know."

Horrified, I looked up from my cup. "What!"

"I mean, there wouldn't have been time for you to get here, but..."

"He asked for... for me?" I could feel tears pricking my eyes, but I refused to cry till I was safely back in Brooklyn. Buffalo had claimed too many of my tears already.

"Well, he asked for Monica. Same thing."

I stood up, feeling suddenly trapped. I could barely breathe.

"I'll be in the greenhouse. Let us know when you're ready to go."

I fled to the sanctuary of glass, that room where so many years ago I had flung myself into the arms of the old man. I had always loved the greenhouse, with its earthy smell. Despite the warmth I shivered, my jacket still downstairs.

Mark and I chatted for a few minutes, covering the highlights and lowlights of the past fifteen years. Marriages, kids, divorces, careers. Soon Allyson appeared with my jacket and bag.

"The cars are loaded. Ready?"

I reached into my bag for the patent pumps I carried with me.

"Ready? Hell no. Not for this. Never for this." I tossed my sneakers into the bag and shrugged my jacket on. "Let's go."

And so we went. The family of florists, the Greek, and the tagalong: Monica.

The backseats and trunks of the four cars were filled with flowers, and I rode with Allyson to the church.

Buffalo had one more ghost. More words left unsaid.

"Did the old man ask for me, Allyson?" I inquired as we drove to the church. "Leo says he asked for me."

"Dad was with him at the end. It all happened pretty fast. He wasn't feeling right and called Dad for help. The next thing Dad knew, he was gone." She shrugged. "I don't know, but I wouldn't be surprised if he had asked for you. He loved his Monica." She made a left turn into the church parking lot. "You stayed in his heart, even after all these years."

Allyson shut the car off. I closed my eyes, trying to block out what we were about to do.

It was time to unload the trunk. So many floral tributes to my beloved Hans.

I steeled my resolve. "Ok, let's do it."

Another body committed to the dark embrace of the soil.

And when the clods of dirt dropped onto the wood of the casket, I threw my rare black rose into the abyss, to be turned back into earth. Just like him.

He was 83 years old.

ACKNOWLEDGEMENTS

There aren't many people I can thank, because no one knew I was writing this. But a few people stand out...

I want to thank the Candyman of Upstate New York. For the red lollipops, for the conversation, and for finding something worthwhile in a young girl.

Many thanks to my beta readers, especially Dan, who read it by accident.

My thanks also extend to my friend and marketing guru, Rachel V.